Camp Cook

Matt Sims

High Noon Books
Novato, California

Editor: Susan Blackaby
Cover Illustration: James Watling
Interior Illustrations: Rick Hackney

International Standard Book Number: 1-57128-275-0

0 9 8 7 6 5 4
0 9 8 7 6 5 4 3

You'll enjoy all the High Noon Books. Write for
a free full list of titles or visit our web site at
www.HighNoonBooks.com.

Contents

No Fun
at Camp

Mark was at Camp Cook. He did not like it a bit. He did not like to hike or swim. He did not like to play sports. He did not like to sing. He did not like to make things.

"This is no fun," said Mark. "I can not take three weeks of this!"

Mark sat on his bunk. It felt like a mound of rocks.

"I hate it here," Mark said.

Mark went to the mess tent. He was in charge of set up for the noon meal. He had to

"I can not take three weeks of this!"
said Mark.

wipe off trays.

Mark did his work. Then he got in line with a tray to get a plate of pork chops and Swiss chard.

Lunch Mate

Mark sat down at the back of the mess tent. A girl with a sad face sat on the edge of the bench. She did not speak.

Mark ate a bite of Swiss Chard. It made him scowl.

"This is not like the food at my house," said Mark.

Then the girl took a bite of her Swiss chard. "Yuck!" she said.

"You need first aid," said Mark. "Have a slurp of milk."

"Boy," said the girl with a sniff. "That Swiss chard is not good."

The girl took a bite of her Swiss chard.
"Yuck!" she said.

"The pork chops and Swiss Chard beats that last dish we had by a mile," said Mark.

"What was that stuff?" said the kid.

"To judge from the scent, it was beans and a large scoop of dirt," said Mark.

The girl had to smile.

Meet Joy

The girl blew her nose.

"Hi," she said. "My name is Joy."

"Hi," said Mark. "My name is Mark. I hate it here. I want to go home."

"Me, too," said Joy.

"Where do you live?" said Mark.

"I live in Grant Park," said Joy.

"Grant Park is home of the best milk shakes in the world," said Mark.

"I know. My dad owns a book shop in town," said Joy. "I wish we were there. I miss

"I live in Grant Park," said Joy.

my mom and dad."

"Me, too," said Mark. "I mean that I wish we were at the shake shop. I do not miss your mom and dad. I miss my mom and dad."

Joy had to smile at the joke Mark made.

Woe Is Mark

"Did I see you on the hike up the gorge?" said Joy.

"Yes," said Mark. "What was the point? You take a look and trudge back."

"It was neat up at

the top," said Joy.

"Yes, but why hike?" said Mark. "You can drive up to the top."

"I see what you mean," said Joy.

"My feet have not felt worse," said Mark.

"Did you dip your feet in the brook?" said Joy.

"Yes, and I got my

socks wet," said Mark.

"Did you like the birds in the woods by the rope bridge?" said Joy.

"The hawks were sort of cool," said Mark.

Mark stood. "It was nice to meet you," he said. "I have no choice. I must now go weave a belt."

"It was nice to meet you," Mark said.

"I have to go, too," said Joy. "I have to carve a trout. Do you want to meet up at free time?"

"Yes," said Mark. "Meet me by the lodge at three."

"I will be there," said Joy.

Fun at Camp

At three, Mark and Joy met on the porch of the lodge.

"Do you want to shoot some hoops?" said Joy.

"Yes," said Mark. "We can play horse."

At three, Mark and Joy met on the porch of the lodge.

"You are on," said Joy. "You can go first."

Mark and Joy were in the mood to goof off. They went to the pool. Then they went to play darts and cards.

At five, Mark said, "I need to go. It is time to set out the forks and spoons for the choice food at the mess tent."

"I will join you at six," said Joy. "I will save you a spot."

"It is a deal," said Mark.

Joy and Mark had fun in the last weeks of camp. They swam. They went on three hikes. They made things. And they sang songs at the camp round up.

Gifts and Good Byes

On the last day, Joy said, "I will miss you. You made camp fun."

"So did you," said Mark.

Joy gave Mark a gift. It was a trout made of wood.

"Wow," said Mark. "It seems real! Did you carve this?"

"Yes," said Joy. "I made it for you."

Mark gave Joy a belt. It had a black hawk in a blue sky on it.

"Wow, this is cool," said Joy.

"I am glad you like it," said Mark.

"Wow," said Mark. "It seems real.
Did you carve this?"

It was time for Joy to get on her bus.

"Send me e-mail," said Joy.

"I will," said Mark. He gave Joy a hug. "I will tell you when I can join you for a shake in Grant Park."

"You have a deal," said Joy. "I will save you a spot."

High Frequency Words

are	said	was
been	some	were
do	the	what
down	there	where
from	they	your
have	to	
of	want	